For Mark, James, Joe and Jess ~ JH
For Matilda Rose, with love ~ VB

LITTLE TIGER PRESS
An imprint of Magi Publications
1 The Coda Centre, 189 Munster Road, London SW6 6AW
www.littletigerpress.com
First published in Great Britain 2009
Text copyright © Julia Hubery 2009
Illustrations copyright © Victoria Ball 2009
Julia Hubery and Victoria Ball have asserted their rights
to be identified as the author and illustrator of this work under the
Copyright, Designs and Patents Act, 1988
A CIP catalogue record for this book is available
from the British Library
All rights reserved • ISBN 978-1-84506-969-8
Printed in China
1 3 5 7 9 10 8 6 4 2

Christmas With You

Julia Hubery

illustrated by
Victoria Ball

LITTLE TIGER PRESS
London

Wide awake when the world is still,

watch the snow fall, soft and slow.

Tiptoe down
to catch
the **thrill,**
our faces
lit by
candle glow.

Eager eyes are shining bright
as papers crackle,
ribbons curl.

Find a shimmering world of white —

swoop and dip and dance and whirl!

Catch a **snowflake** on your nose,

make an **angel**,

make a **friend**.

Run and toast our
tingling toes,

wish today would **never** end!

Luscious,
scrumptious,
richly sumptuous,

fun and feasting all together.

Playing games with clues that send us

racing for the
hidden treasure.

Fly on wings of ice, so daring,

till we tumble in surprise!

Voices bright, with lanterns flaring –

sing out under crystal skies!

After all the celebrating,

up the stairs we softly tread . . .

There we'll find a warm bed waiting,
there we'll lay your sleepy head.

So close your eyes, and drift away

in tender dreams
of Christmas Day.